The Whale Culture of Greenland

Kai Kean

The Whale Culture of Greenland

The Voyages of Vito de la Vera

Counterfactual Archeology

Editor: Kai Kean
Proof reading: Kai Kean

Publisher: BoD – Books on Demand, Hellerup, Denmark

Printing: BoD – Books on Demand, Norderstedt, Germany

ISBN: 9788743044680

§ § §

Archeology is special among the sciences. One does not necessarily know what one is looking for and even less what one finds. Everything you thought you knew can change with just a single find that changes everything.

This is how I came here to Scoresbyland in Northeast Greenland.

Much is known about the Inuit and Thule culture, which spread in the Arctic archipelago and Greenland seven hundred years ago and is still the origin of today's Inuit culture.

But before that, there was another culture up here in the Arctic. A much older culture, which we call the Dorset culture. Our museums have objects from this culture, which count between 1000 and 2000, but since the culture was already fading away when the Thule culture came along with the small ice age, it is sparse what we know about them.

During his Thule expeditions among the Inuit, the well-known Knud Rasmussen heard legends about the long-gone "Tunit". Giants of the past who had disappeared with the advent of the Inuit. The Tunit, however, has left many traces.

They lived in houses, so you can find in the Arctic ruins from the Tunit settlements, which were also excavated by Therkel Mathiasen during the Thule expeditions.

There are many indications that the Dorset culture was in its last phase long before the Thule culture came and that they were not as well adapted to the colder climate as the Inuit. Their time was from before the Little Ice Age, when the Arctic was more hospitable.

And now climate change is loosening up for the Arctic again, more and more of the Tunit cultural remnants are being brought to light again.

Among other things, many petroglyphs have been found, which we also know from Denmark's antiquity.

The Dorset culture has left many behind and they are one of the most emphatic memories of them.

It is also petroglyphs that have brought me here to Scoresbyland, where I, who write these words, am not far from Zackenberg station, where these special petroglyphs were recently found, which others unfortunately have not taken so much notice of, but I think they are of utmost importance!

Normally, the oldest of the Dorset culture is set to 1000-800 BC, but the culture took long to die and was not as well adapted to the cold Arctic as the Thule culture that followed it. Therefore, the compelling question of whether the Dorset culture was the slow adaptation and death of an Arctic culture that was even older but adapted to a warmer Arctic arise.

Much could indicate that the Dorset culture is the remnants of a culture around the Arctic Ocean, which has had its peak during the Holocene maximum around 5000-2000 BC. During this warm period, the Arctic Ocean would have been ice-free and far more hospitable, which is why it would also be able to support a different type of culture.

This is what I have found indications for and the reason that I am now here in Scoresbyland to examine the petroglyphs. Evidence that during the Holocene maximum there was an Arctic culture that was contemporaneous with our Bronze Age and which slowly degenerated and fled south under the colder conditions until the Little Ice Age finally ended the sad remnants of their culture.

My journey is going well. Scoresbyland has a beautiful Arctic summer and I was able to sail my yacht L'Aguila here with a stop in Scoresbysund, where I stocked up.

There were no major problems in the sailing, as the East Greenlandic ocean ice is not what it has been. It almost gives an insight into how the sea was for the Holocene culture in the Arctic.

The sea would have been rich and provided what was needed. Like all Arctic cultures, even in warmer conditions, the Holocene culture must have depended on the sea and grazing animals on land.

The question then is how developed it was. Have they perhaps had some form of aquaculture? It thrives in Arctic waters. I put my trust in the petroglyphs that they can show me something.

In the Scoresby plains, the musk oxen graze well contented in the abundance of the Arctic summer. Further down in the fjords, the whales' large fins and backs appear from time to time when they break the water surface.

This is what one should always remember about the Arctic. The inconsolability of winter is replaced by the abundance of summer, as long as the sun stands forever in the sky and the light bathes the landscape in its rays.

The arctic flora is in full bloom around me and provides abundant food for musk oxen, reindeer, insects and birds. The short growth period only makes the explosion of life so much more impressive when all the flowers are blooming at the same time.

It is not necessarily all a benefit to me as there are many insects in the air. The mosquitoes are fierce, but I have the classic Greenlandic mosquito net over my head and face, so I do not quite end up as a buffet.

The rocks protrude everywhere in the landscape, while the rivers with meltwater run between them.

The Arctic summer offers plenty of good weather. It's only sometimes that the weather gets bad, but then it's really bad!

Finally, I see the cliff that I am looking for. It is a large slightly sloping rock wall in the landscape. It has a huge, easily accessible surface to carve in, as the ancient Tunit did.

I run fast towards my goal full of anticipation. This is what I've been looking for!

It is true! The rock is filled with petroglyphs, the entire surface has incisions! I can hardly believe it!

I put my pack down and immediately start unpacking. Paint, brushes, charcoal, tracing paper and a camera.

First the paint! I grab a brush and open a bucket of paint. The petroglyphs only become clear and fully visible when they are painted up, otherwise they are just scratches in the rock, even though the artists here in their time have chosen rocks where the surface is colored differently than the interior due to exposure to wind and weather. So when they were made, they were completely visible. But that's a long time ago. Wind and weather have long changed that.

I will make up for that soon! I use paint, which becomes luminescent in the dark. It does not make much sense now in the summer, but if you come back when the season of darkness has come, the petroglyphs will shine. A pretty good idea I think to myself.

I'm getting off to a good start painting. And some forms also make sense. I'm sure these round horned figures are the musk oxen that graze nearby. And whale tails as we ourselves reproduce them. And matchmen have always been made.

It's a wealth of characters. Some are more stylized than others. It could almost be a pictorial writing.

For me, though, the actual pictures are most helpful. The whale has clearly had great importance for the Holocene culture as a resource base. A single whale has made up a huge amount of resources in terms of food, fat and oil for heating and cooking. In addition, skins and bones for tools.

The whale has no doubt been of great importance with all the pictures I find. And strange vessels they have chased them in. One has a ellipse above the boat. Wonder what it signifies?

However, the whale does not stand alone. Fish and seaweed are also there and of course the seal stands out prominently. Many of the pictures are easy to decipher. An image speaks both across time and culture.

Of land animals, both the musk ox and the reindeer have given rise to many images and I have also found Nanoq, the mighty polar bear who, as in the current Inuit culture, has instilled awe.

I paint many petroglyphs, but it still forms only a small part of the large rock.

There is work here for a long time, but I feel confirmed that there really has been a past culture around the Arctic Ocean during the Holocene maximum and it may very well be the distant origin of the Dorset culture.

There are many markings of boats, so they have been oriented to the sea. The boats were made of bones and skins. On the whole, there is a lot that indicates that they have worked a lot in animal products for their homes, vessels and tools. Thus I find a carving resembling a hall built of the ribs of a whale. It must have been a communal house of some kind.

That may explain why so little has been found of them. If most of it has been made from animal products, it's long gone. Only the bones will in any sense be able to remain and much of them have probably ended up in the sea.

But what is carved in stone is far more durable, as all these petroglyphs are a clear sign of.

There must also be foundations of peat huts in some places, which have been found after the Dorset culture, but it requires that you find them and here there are no locals who have just passed them, as Knud Rasmussen found it on the 5th Thule expedition. However, I do not see any peat huts in the petroglyphs that I have painted. Were peat huts perhaps a development for a colder climate?

It's hard to paint the whole day, even though it's bright around the clock, you still have to sleep at so point not to mention getting some food. It is fortunate that the cliff is so close to the fjord that I can return aboard L'Aguila when I am tired. It would be unsafe to sleep alone in the wilderness if a polar bear were to come to visit.

I pack up and just want to take a picture of my progress, but the camera does not work. That's typical! Best as one would use it! Well, luckily I have plenty of tracing paper for markings, but it's slavish.

I return to the fjord, where L'Aguila is anchored. I have pulled my small rowing boat ashore. I get it in the water and turn the little engine on and return to L'Aguila. She's my second home. It's always nice to get on board. I put some food over and get some time to write these lines about the day's work. I feel relieved to see so much evidence that I am right that the Arctic has been populated long before history would normally have it. Many historians are reluctant to accept that there may be older cultures outside the common ones. They have forgotten that history is also about discovering new things, even if one deals with the past. Many are directly reluctant to acknowledge Greenland's deeper prehistory.

Here, archeology should be able to step in when historians only want to look at written sources, but far too many archaeologists just want to preserve known domestic things or dig where others have dug before and there are comfortable hotels nearby. Really to go out and find new old things and risk stepping on some toes that could give promotions, is not desired. I could not even find a single one who would accompany me on my journey here. It was perceived as ridiculous!

Fortunately, I have the funds to self-finance, as there was not much desire to support me in my efforts.

It is sad that it is so, but it must not hinder the work. Once I have slept, I will continue working.

I'm back at the cliff. The sun is in the north, so it is in the strictest sense night, but it does not matter up here. You sleep when you are tired.

Work with the paintbrush again! There is enough to tackle when painting up the past. There are an incredible number of petroglyphs on this rock. It is almost a library left by this distant and forgotten culture. I find several of the strange boats with ellipses above.

They appear to be chasing whales and other animals from it. Oddly enough, there is a picture where they are also hunting musk oxen. An artist is known to take liberties, but the harpoon was certainly a favored weapon.

There are also carvings that are definitely qulliq or blubber lamps. It is very natural in a world without wood. The blubber lamps are also pictured with other constructions that it must have been used with. Whale blubber has a much higher calorific value than wood, so in a world where access to it has been good, one has also had plenty of energy available.

In any case, it seems that they have used the heat from the blubber lamps to blow things up and get air up to speed.

The picture that emerges for me is certainly of a more advanced culture that thrived in the warmer Arctic climate during the Holocene maximum. The ensuing cold has certainly pushed this culture back hard until it became the Dorset culture as we know it. The Tunit people have thus been pushed south and has survived there under far harsher conditions than their ancestors, who had the surplus to chisel down so much of themselves on this cliff.

It seems to me that part of what I am painting here is also an instruction on how to make different remedies. It may be that it has even been used for teaching. It is at least detailed how a whale hall could have been constructed from the whale's ribs covered with skins and with belly skins as windows. There have been entire bone towns where the distant Tunit have lived and these halls have been able to be packed down so that the towns could follow the catch in the strange boats. All transport would be by sea. There were no dogs for transport, as we otherwise know the Arctic today, but it was not pronounced in the later Dorset culture either.

I paint what most resembles a drawing of a Tunit city. There are the halls made of whale ribs set in a star shape, where the halls radiate from a central square. Near I see several of the boats with the strange ellipse above and most remarkably there is a bonfire on board the boats. It is very strange that they should have blubber lamps on board with the risk of fire. Nevertheless, the symbols fit. And again carvings show hunting of musk oxen from the boats.

It could be exciting to explore the area and see if there might be other signs of the Holocene Tunit than just these petroglyphs. They must have returned here often to carve more pictures into the rock and tell their story for posterity.

It is thought-provoking how few traces a culture can leave behind, so it becomes as if they had never been here. If enough time had passed, these carvings would also have been worn away from the rock and nothing would be left.

I am struck by a curiosity that makes me put down the brush and start walking in the magnificent nature that surrounds me. It feels completely untouched by humans, which it also has been for several hundred years until the arrival of Norwegian fur hunters, which led to the Danish government's establishment of Scoresbysund to maintain claims on Northeast Greenland. Something that still requires maintenance by patrolling with the Sirius Patrol even in winter, when other countries are pulling their patrols south.

I stay a little further up in relation to the sea. As Therkel Mathiasen found during Knud Rasmussen's expedition, the Tunit people's settlements were high above the water as the water level subsequently fell and the land rose. It goes without saying that the land has risen a lot since the Holocene maximum and at the same time the water level has been higher during this warm period.

This is also seen at the Bronze Age town of Ur in Mesopotamia, which today lies deep inland but was then a port city. Thus, I also have to find signs of settlements higher up on land here.

I follow the landscape along a cliff edge that may have been the shoreline at the time. I'm hoping to find something this close to the rock with the petroglyphs.

Of course, it's a waste of time to interrupt my work with the petroglyphs to go around looking for something I do not know if I will find, but I feel that the petroglyphs have given me an idea of what to look for. If there are bones from sea creatures all the way up here, they must have been brought here by someone at a time when the sea was closer, so I have to keep an eye out. Hopefully there are some places where a layer of peat has not grown over the archaeological finds.

I find a high place where I get a view of the area. Over there I see the rock with my paintings of petroglyphs. There is still a lot of paint work waiting. Down in the fjord I can see L'Aguila lying in the calm water and on the plain grazing reindeer and musk oxen.

I look back at the rock with the petroglyphs. Where would it make sense to have a camp in relation to the cliff? I let my eyes glide across the landscape and the elevation that has been coastline in the distant past.

There is an elevation in the landscape that rises easily at a suitable distance from the coast. It could be a good option. I decide to try to go there. There is also something in the peat there. These may be the leftovers I'm looking for.

It is a brisk quick walk from the vantage point to the elevation, which is at a meaningful distance from the rock with petroglyphs.

I reach the elevation and soon stand on it and see to my delight that there really are bone remains here! The peat layer is thin, so the layer has not been able to cover the bone remains.

I grab a bone and lift it up from the peat. It's really a whale rib right up here from the sea! It can only have been brought here! It quickly becomes clear that there are several whale bones on the site. Of course, millennia of wind, weather and animals mean that there is not much system in it, but nevertheless there are bones here that give an idea that there has been a larger settlement in this place.

I sit down and contemplate the star-shaped setting of whale halls that must have been here in the distant past and how little is left of these people. If it had not been for the petroglyphs, I would hardly have thought further about slightly scattered bones here on the elevation or would have gone up to the vantage point to look for white bones in the peat.

Now, in addition to the rock with petroglyphs, I also have an excavation site. Of course, some whale ribs and bones do not prove much, but there may be something more descriptive to be found.

I look a little at the whale rib and notice that notches have been made in it. It has no doubt been to keep the skin stretched across it. It is a small proof of tools.

I walk around the mound a bit and find little things in bones too, but these distant people have been good at not leaving much behind. They must have used almost everything and therefore there is not much left either. It is often waste heaps that gives the best finds, as we know it from Ertebølle. But if everything from the prey has been used and has been worn out completely, it will be difficult to find remains.

At least I found this place. I take the rib and the other little things with me. I will focus on the petroglyphs on the rock and return to this once I have painted everything. If only the stupid camera worked! First I go down to the fjord and put my finds in the small boat. I still have time to work a little up the cliff, so I hurry up there.

From the cliff I can see the elevation where the settlement has been. It's just a short distance. They have been able to view the cliff from the settlement when it was inhabited.

I wonder if there are no more rocks like this at other settlements that they must have had when they followed the prey?

And there must have been other tribes who have had theirs. How widespread was this culture? Did it surround the entire Arctic Ocean? Where did it originate and spread from? The questions arise and stand in line, but I have to find the answers little by little.

I paint several petroglyphs of blubber lamps. It is quite clear that it has been central to the culture. Something could indicate that it has been before the Saqqaq culture in West Greenland. Perhaps it has even spread from the Holocene culture to the Saqqaq culture and on to the Dorset culture. There may therefore be a connection between the Holocene culture and the Independence I culture and the Saqqaq culture, which has subsequently passed into the Independence II culture and over to the Dorset culture. Thus, these cultures, if descended from the Holocene culture, came from the north after the Holocene maximum.

Normally, blubber lamps are considered to have originated in the West Greenlandic Saqqaq culture approx. 4000 years ago, but this could indicate that it came from the north from the Holocene culture as it went south.

However, it seems from the petroglyphs that the blubber lamps in the Holocene culture were made of bone like everything else. It was not a stone culture. Their blubber lamps appear from the petroglyphs to be made of hollowed-out bones, which have also made it possible to direct the heat and fire.

Perhaps the blubber lamps in soapstone, as they are known from the Saqqaq culture, have been inspired by the older bone blubber lamps that came from the north. Soapstones may have replaced bones due to poorer whaling, which has been important for the Holocene culture to get bones that were large enough for their blubber lamps.

Lack of whale bones has also made it difficult to make the boat types that I find in the petroglyphs. This deficiency may explain the decline in material culture that must be have been from the whale culture to the Independence cultures and the Saqqaq culture, where an adaptation has then taken place with the Dorset culture.

The end of the Holocene maximum has simply forced the culture south and away from the Arctic Ocean and in the process they have lost the opportunity to catch enough whales to maintain a whale-based culture as a source of raw materials.

The whale culture has thus been destroyed by the progress of the ice, which has increased the dependence on land animals, as seen in the Independence cultures, which were based on land hunting. During the Holocene maximum, whales could be hunted all year round.

The big question is how the whale culture moved south and became the Dorset culture via the Independence culture and the Saqqaq culture.

It must have been an abrupt change in climate that reduced whale culture's oceanic orientation to the more land-based Independence I culture. But if access to resources has been interrupted by a colder climate, then the culture has also perished relatively quickly and there are not many remnants because it was based on animal products rather than stones.

The whole part of the rock that I have painted up now seems to be about blubber lamps, where the variation has been very great. Blubber lamps are perhaps much to say. They do not quite look like the lamps we know from later cultures, but they are based on blubber, that much is clear. It is the only fuel that the Arctic makes abundantly available.

The whale culture has had many blubber lamps made of hollowed bones and the whale ribs, where fire and heat have been able to be concentrated in a jet upwards through the bone.

They thus seem to have been very adept at focusing fire and heat in a specific direction. Therefore, they must also have had great control over where and for what they wanted to apply the heat from the blubber.

I paint a petroglyph showing one of the elongated blubber lamps blowing up a skin. They have been able to make skin or intestinal skin balloons! It's unbelievable!

By focusing the heat from the blubber lamps, they have simply been able to make hot air balloons. It is an incredible achievement all the way back in the Stone and Bronze Ages to be able to make hot air balloons.

I have to sit down and let it sink in. This culture all the way up here in the far north was able to make hot air balloons!

After some time in thought, it actually makes sense. With their abundant access to blubber, they have had access to the most concentrated fuel of the time. And everything else they needed they also had directly from their prey and as long as the catch was good, they would have ample time in surplus to develop things. They had no fields that required all their time and effort.

But then it must also mean that the strange boats with ellipses above have been hot air balloons with gondolas below. They have chased from the air! It also explains that they were depicted hunting terrestrial animals as well. From the air you can hunt both on land and at sea.

And as they could make a concentrated jet with their blubber lamps, they have also been able to make propulsion in their airships.

I'm completely stunned. This is more than I could ever have expected when I came up here to study the petroglyphs. To think of such an advanced culture that has existed up here so long ago far from the known cultures.

It suddenly strikes me that when the whale culture was able to sail the Arctic sky after whales, then the sea has not posed any major barrier to them. In the air, they have been able to reach all the shores around the Arctic Ocean in their search for the large marine mammals. They have been limited only by the distribution of their primary catch.

18

It is almost unbelievable that such a culture could have existed up here, but when only the climatic conditions were more favorable.

It also strikes me that as they have been able to travel across both water and land, then the whale culture does not have to have come from the south via the Arctic archipelago. It may have spread directly along the shores of the Arctic Ocean or even across the Arctic Ocean! Where did they originally originate?

This question is on my mind while I am back on board l'Aguila. I have an idea of what happened to the whale culture after the Holocene maximum. They decayed with the colder climate and became the Tunit people and the Dorset culture via the Independence cultures and the Saqqaq culture. But where did they come from? They have originated and have spread across the Arctic Ocean in their airships, but where was the stone for this culture laid? I can not deduce this from the petroglyphs here at the end of the world, but I can speculate. Their culture was so dependent on whales for their technology that it must have evolved where there has been good access to this large marine mammal. And with good access, I mean they must have been easy to catch. From there, they must have spread around the Arctic Ocean.

It is clear to me that when I finish researching and documenting the petroglyphs here, I will have to search for reports of similar petroglyphs and finds of large quantities of whale bones. This should put me on the trail to areas where the whale culture has been established.

I sit on the deck and look in at the shore that stretches around me. Only up here in the rich Arctic waters could such an advanced culture emerge on the basis of hunting rather than agriculture. It is a completely different way of establishing such a culture with a high technical level than what we are familiar with.

Such a culture must also have developed and spread over a long period of time until it has filled the areas where that technology was usable. The whale culture has, by its nature, not been able to spread away from the rich northern seas with ample access to marine mammals, as they would then no longer be able to find the resources on which their culture was based. And when the cold came after the Holocene maximum, it was also their downfall. The easy access to their raw materials disappeared and pulled the rug away under their culture.

They must have been established in a place where the new warmer conditions of the Arctic Ocean have become accessible and where at the same time there were a population that could spread there and were accustomed to the more Arctic or colder seas.

This has at least given me a goal to continue my work when I return from here. Similar petroglyphs must have been described elsewhere.

In the fjord I see a whale's ridge coming up above the surface. Here in the summer period, they are plentiful. But in the winter, the ice will close the area all the way down the east coast and around Cape Farewell. It is the winter conditions that have been too much for the whale culture.

During the Holocene maximum, the sea was still accessible in winter, enabling access to the vital blubber. Without it no whale culture. It is disturbing to think about how dependent a culture can be on a single product and when it is gone, the culture is too.

After another light sleep, I walk back up to my cliff, which is starting to get pretty colorful. I'm glad I brought plenty of paint. And in many colors, so that the rock now has different petroglyphs painted up in different colors. By color-coding uniform petroglyphs, I find it easier to locate them when I want to return to compare with others that I find later. Then I can take a copy and lay next to it to see the degree of uniformity. Thereby I can also see the development in the way individual concepts are depicted.

There are clear developments in the stylization that carry towards a pictorial writing that, however, still leaves recognizability. That's lucky for me. It gives me an opportunity to read the pictures.

There is a clear indication of a development of the carvings over time, where it becomes clear that some ideas such as musk ox, fire, whale, seal, polar bear, etc., which are widely used, develop into simple and rapid carvings, which have been known to all.

Here, too, I see clearly that I have not begun from the beginning on the cliff, but somewhere in the middle of the development, where some signs were incomprehensible, until I found an older more pictorial rendering.

I have now reached about two-thirds of the rock carvings of the rock. It's a big job and I have not been able to make sense of everything I have painted, but I have gained a really good insight into the Holocene culture, which I now call the whale culture.

Many of the pictures are instructions about the material culture, but there is also a lot that must refer to religious beliefs and some that I am hopeful about that they show the story of how the whale people got here. There is something in it that gives me a feeling that they have reached this point in their airships over water and not from the west over land.

Is it possible that they have flown over the Northern Ocean and reached here from Svalbard? As far as I know, no archaeological finds have been made on Svalbard, but that does not say much, as the whale culture has left so few indications of their existence. Perhaps they came from the archipelagos and the coast north of Siberia and came here via Svalbard.

The Russians' unwillingness to let foreigners come to their Arctic coast and the limited study of the same could easily mean that there are as yet undiscovered cultural layers in northern Siberia and along the Arctic Ocean.

It could then be that the whale culture has spread along the Siberian coast and out on the Arctic islands and all the way here to Northeast Greenland and perhaps eventually stumbled upon itself again as it has spread to the Arctic archipelago and Canada. With access to airships, it is not an unthinkable development and the culture has spread along the coasts and seas, where the important whaling has been good and plentiful.

Russia will not be easy in terms of further investigations, but perhaps there are descriptions of finds along the Siberian coast and to Svalbard I have access if there are descriptions of something and it should be available in Norwegian.

If the whale culture has spread both east and west along the Arctic Ocean, there should also be descriptions to be found. There are many possibilities and a lot of work to find other people's descriptions, but so far the rock gives me hope.

There are several petroglyphs indicating that the whale culture has come from the east. The pictures show them coming with the rising sun in the back and with the setting sun in front. Those who have settled here in Scorebyland have thus come here from the east, where they also depict that they have come across a large sea in their airships in search of the whales, whose migration led them here. It is clearly marked that where the whales went, the whale culture followed. The whale culture was therefore defined by the whales' migrations in the Arctic Ocean.

Like the Thule culture and the Inuit of today, who worshiped the great mother of the sea, so too has the whale culture had a worship of the sea, from which the important whales and to some extent also seals and walrus came.

I find several petroglyphs of a person depicted under the sea with hands outstretched, from which whales, seals and fish flow out and up to the people waiting over the water in their airships.

Above them, the sun keeps the clouds and wind away, so it is cloudless and windless. These have, of course, been important conditions for the whale culture, as strong winds have been able to blow them hard off course and make landing almost impossible.

Even today, the vast majority of days up here are clear and quiet, interrupted only by a few but severe storms and heavy rainfall. It is highly conceivable that during the Holocene maximum there have been even more clear and quiet days in the milder climate, but all the more so the storms have been terrible for the whale culture. They have been few, but when they came, the airships have been in great danger if they were in the air or on their way up or down. Therefore, high and clear sunny weather was been paramount.

Many of the petroglyphs here among the religious motifs also give an indication that evil has been represented by storms and winds. The worst that culture could imagine. It can hardly have taken much wind before landing the airships has become very difficult without damage.

The very good weather in the Arctic and few but strong storms have certainly been an advantage, but also put a limit on the whale culture's ability to stretch south. Their airships have not had it easy if they had landed in the dominant wind belts that we know from Denmark and the North Atlantic. The weather has therefore also put a limit on the whale culture's ability to spread.

A clear picture is formed of a culture with an idea of the rewarding sea and the good sun, which forms the framework of an orderly and calm world, which is disturbed by wind spirits and impassable mountains inland. The whale culture has probably stuck to the coastal plains, as here in Scoresbyland, where they have been able to hunt reindeer and musk without getting too far inland, where sudden gusts of wind can occur among the mountains.

Like many other ancient cultures, the whale culture has had a clear division between order and chaos. Where calm weather has been order and storm has been chaos and as Knud Rasmussen found among Thule culture's Inuit, it was probably also important in the whale culture to abide by taboos, so that no disorder arose with all the resulting injuries and ills.

Of course, I can not definitively deduce this from the petroglyphs, but it is very logical to reach that conclusion, as it aligns with other societies that have been subject to the whims of the weather. There are also carvings that show people kneeling for what must be mountain and sea spirits, so that these all will remain satisfied and not quarrel, so that the winds rise.

I've come as far as I can this day, so I go back once more and sail out on L'Aguila to get myself some well-deserved rest. I decide to return to where the settlement has been. It may be that I can find something more there once I have rested.

But first I sit down and write this and consider what places I can search for accounts of finds that may relate to the whale culture and my further account of this.

Oslo is an option if there are documents on something from Longyearbyen on Svalbard. I decide to link up to the internet via my Iridium connection. Satellite links are expensive, but I think it's worth it to take a quick look at whether there are any reports from the archives in Oslo.

It took some time, but it turned out that there was a note from one of the Fram expeditions about a cliff with strange carvings, which they had visited on the basis of a report from a whaler who had been at anchor there. I quickly write the position down. It is a later place to visit. Now I have something to move on with.

I turn off the computer and go to rest.

Immediately after breakfast I go ashore again and go straight up to the hilltop where I found the whale rib. I am convinced that it is the right place for a settlement. So I immediately set about exploring the place. The peat layer in Greenland is formed very slowly, so the bedrock is not far below the grass.

The whale culture has not left much for posterity. To that extent, it has not been a use and throw away culture. To my great delight, however, I find a splinter of bone that must have been a sewing needle. It may have been lost at some point and therefore not brought along. However, there is not much left to find here. I therefore decide to try with a little digging and take out my field shovel and start scraping away the peat layer.

The rock is just below, so I don't get too much excavation work.

Suddenly it strikes me that I should try to dig the peat away where I found the whale rib.

I go there and start scraping the peat around the rib marking away. Then I encounter a depression in the rock around the same width as the rib.

For a moment I ponder the meaning, but then it strikes me. If this has been a permanent residence, then they have made recesses to put their whale halls up in! That must be it!

I dig the depression completely free. It is a fine and regular depression. It bears the mark of being processed. They probably burned blubber to heat the rock so that it broke, after which they worked loose stones out and then burned again until they had the desired depression to plant their whale halls in.

I start from the depression I have found and dig in the directions that make the best sense for a rectangular hall located along with other halls in a star shape from the center.

To my great delight, I soon dig out more depressions. They are in a row with about one meter to one and a half in between and two meters inwards. It's a lot like I saw on the petroglyphs!

They have not left much behind in the material sense, but their carvings in the rock show their existence!

Soon I have exposed the entire foundation of the hall. It has been two meters wide and eight meters long. I smile to myself. This clearly shows a correspondence between the petroglyphs and the archaeological realities. So the airships can also be a reality.

I started from the end of the hall, which must have turned inward into the star shape to find depressions for the other halls. It does not take long, then I have found the next and the next. There have been eight whale halls that have gone out from the center and formed an eight-pointed star here on the mound with good views of the sea. It's a huge success! I have found unequivocal remnants!

I bring the whale rib that I first found back to the site and put it down in the depression. It slides straight down and stands by itself. Together with those who have been in the other depressions, they have formed pillars that bend slightly inward. They must then have somehow been connected inwards in the middle, so that the hall has been given structure, but it is quite clear that the ribs have been used in this way. Here they have been mounted in the depressions in the rock, but where the peat has been deeper, the ribs have no doubt been able to be knocked down so that they stood. It must have been the solution for temporary settlements that have not been used over and over again.

It strikes me that I am fortunate that there has been an elevation here that has been obvious to use over and over again, so it has made sense to spend time and energy making the recesses that I have then been able to find.

I have brought some marking poles, which I now mount in all the depressions, so I get a clear overview of the settlement's structure.

It amazes me that the whale culture has otherwise been so good at avoiding leaving something behind that they have then left this rib behind. The bone needle is easily lost, but the rib is noticeable, so why was it left? It has been left at a time when they have not returned. Of course, I can only guess. It has at least been left behind, even if there is so little else.

I keep walking around and researching the settlement. It has been cleaned up really well.

I walk a around the settlement. It may be that there are some remains of a waste heap, which are good sources of finds, as we know it from Ertebølle by the Limfjord. If I can find the whale people's kitchen waste, I might find a treasure trove. Since the peat layer is thin, I should be able to see if there is an accumulation near the settlement.

I walk around the settlement in circles, which I continually expand to cover the area as best I can, but I find nothing. Have they really not had a waste heap? That can not be true. I look out towards the fjord, which must have reached all the way to the mound when it was inhabited. Maybe they have thrown it in the sea, then all traces have been deleted and it would be a hygienic benefit to them if the waste simply washed away. It almost has to be. This is how the settlement has been kept clean and tidy.

I go back to the depressions at the top of the mound. If I scrape the whole top free of peat layers, I probably get the best chance of finding anything. There's a bit of work in it, but the layer is thin so it won't take me any longer than until I return to L'Aguila to sleep again.

I manage to expose the rest of the cliff below the top of the mound. I also find a few other bone fragments, one of which could be the tip of a harpoon, but it is very little. The rib remains my biggest find.

It's clear to me that I will not find more here on the mound, but I am now actually quite satisfied. The depressions are clear evidence of a settlement and I had not expected to find it when I came up here to examine the rock with the rock petroglyphs.

I return aboard L'Aguila and catalog my few finds and put them in storage. Tomorrow I can proceed with painting the petroglyphs. On the mound I have found what I can.

The next day I return to the rock with the petroglyphs. All the colors from my paintings make it completely vivid to look at. I have come a long way, but there is still something left that can show me more about the Holocene whale culture and its mysteries.

I'm excited to get started again. It's a shame the camera doesn't work, but then I have to draw it up instead. I'm getting well ahead and now find what looks like funeral ceremonies. What have they done with their dead, now that so few traces are left? The answer comes quickly and fits with my idea of what they did to all the other leftovers.

They bring the dead down to the giving sea, which now receives the dead as an atonement for what he has received from the sea in the course of life. It's a pretty obvious cycle that is being laid out here. What the sea has given is given back again.

From further petroglyphs it soon becomes clear that it has been general, when something has ceased its use, then it has been given back to the great sea. So there is hardly any chance of finding a waste heap here. They have given everything back to the sea. So what can be found is only what has been lost or left behind.

This makes it somewhat more difficult to find remnants of the whale culture and probably also contributes to it being archaeologically unknown. But just because a culture does not leave clear and comprehensive traces, it does not make it any less real.

Fortunately, they have carved tracks in the bedrock, which I can now uncover. A highly mobile culture that has traveled by airship along the Arctic Ocean and has hunted the sea and the country's animals from above. From these animals they have then produced all their material necessities.

All indications are that the use of stones for tools has been virtually unknown. Blubber lamps, which have been found in the later Saqqaq culture, must therefore be a development in this culture. Possibly inspired by the blubber lamps in bones that have driven the whale culture.

I wonder what background the whale culture may have had, since it has so almost completely failed to use stone as a cultural material other than to carve petroglyphs or depressions in? Where did they come from that they did not use stones for their tools, but only products that they were able to extract from their prey? What connection back in their cultural past may have led to this?

I will hardly find that out here, but it strikes me that it is the sea as the origin of all resources that is a recurring image. The hunt for land animals seems to be secondary and perhaps newer. Can there be an answer in this? Has the origin of the whale culture been even more tied to the sea than what is shown in the petroglyphs, which must be a late step in the culture before its decline towards the Independence and Saqqaq cultures?

Many considerations appear to me as I head back to L'Aguila to find some rest after the hardships of the day.

While eating my well-deserved dinner, I look at the position on Svalbard, which I previously wrote down. Once I'm done here and have been home to find further possible stories, it may very well become my next goal.

On Svalbard there were no Inuit cultures afterwards, so here the whale culture went extinct without being followed before we arrived in the islands. This is practical, because there it will be proven that finds do not belong to any later cultural layer, but will come entirely from a now extinct culture.

There is no doubt that this must be the next stop on my travels. First, though, I have to return home to process all that I bring from Scoresbyland.

The rock with the petroglyphs is a pure goldmine and has given me a picture of this now extinct culture, which has been so advanced and yet has left such a limited imprint on the world.

It is thought-provoking that there may be so few remnants of past cultures that our picture of history is in many ways skewed because we do not see those who have not left clear edifices and our search is focused on resident farming cultures. It can create a bias that makes us not see cultures that have been based on hunting, but still very advanced, because hunting has been an abundance industry, as has been the case for the whale culture before its decline.

I look forward to doing more research into stories that can provide ideas about other areas that have been inhabited by the whale culture when I get home. It will certainly be a demanding work to read through expedition diaries in search of small references to petroglyphs on rocks, but it pays off in terms of forming a picture of the spread of culture.

It is my conviction that during the Holocene maximum it must have been able to surround the entire Arctic Ocean and the north-facing shores of the surrounding islands.

The weakness of the culture has been that it has become dependent on the open sea and calm weather conditions during the Holocene maximum, so when the Arctic has become colder again, it has been too fast for them to be able to adapt and the whales have become more difficult to hunt, which has destroyed the material basis of the culture and the airships have disappeared along with the materials from which they were built.

The culture has become more dependent on land prey, as seen in the Independence cultures. The descendants of the whale culture have thus become the Dorset culture and the Tunit culture via the Independence cultures and the Saqqaq culture, which, in the absence of the previously rich resources of whale bones, have begun to use stones for blubber lamps and other tools.

Thus, the whale culture flourished in the Arctic during a rich period between the last ice age and the colder period that followed the Holocene maximum in historical time. It is a thought-provoking tale of how important the climatic conditions are for the existence of a culture. For the whale culture, the rewarding hands of the sea closed with devastating consequences.

The time aboard L'Aguila allows me to digest all such impressions, but I have to make sure to get some sleep even though the sun is shining to the north.

After a well-deserved sleep, I go ashore again. By now there is not much of the rock that I have not painted and I feel like I have built up a picture of an amazing culture that lived here so long ago. I've got a glimpse into their bygone world, but there's still so much hidden in the mists of time. In particular, I have become curious about where this culture may have come from before it reached Scoresbyland here in Greenland?

There is so much substance for my later travels where I hope to be able to clarify other places that have been inhabited by this culture that was so dependent on the giants of the sea that they chased from the air.

I begin painting the petroglyphs on the remaining rock. Maybe I will be lucky enough to find carvings that can point towards the end of this culture. As they have carved the story of their lives into the rock, it could be that they had also carved the story of their death for posterity.

However, I am disappointed. All I find are several reproductions of sacrifices to the sea and the hunting of whales.

But how would I find their decline and disappearance reproduced? How would they show it in pictures on the cliff? Of course I do not know! All I find is what I have already found. The petroglyphs recur. Which is a good thing for knowing the imagery, but I was hoping to find something new.

I sit down below the cliff and look up at the painted surface. I've come a long way. There are less than a tenth left now. Soon the time will come for my departure.

It makes me a little sad. It's a beautiful place, but I do not want to be here, when winter closes its icy grip on this place. The icy grip that also brought the whale culture to an end when the warm weather was over.

I get up and take the rifle over my shoulder to go for a walk in the area. Sometimes it's best to just walk around to clear your mind.

The sun shines down on the grassy river valleys, where the birds fly around and catch insects in the air. The Arctic can be a pure mosquito and fly hell around August, but therefore also a bonanza for birds that enjoy that delicacy. Everything has to happen fast in the short summer, which is rich and rewarding until the sun goes down again.

Even in the time of whale culture, the sun has gone away in the winter months. This they have had to go through even though the weather was warmer. How have they coped through the dark season, when the sun has let them down and they have had a hard time seeing their prey from the airships? Have they had supplies from the summer to make it through the darkness? Or have they sought to the south, where some day has given light in the darkness? They would hardly have done so if they were on Svalbard, but here in Greenland they have been able to go south.

I have not found petroglyphs that have given me any answer to that question. And yet it is an important question. How did they make it through the darkness?

The later cultures did and do catch from the sea ice, but it has not been easy in the warmer climate of the whale culture, where the sea ice has not been a stable occurence.

I have found a considerable additional question to which I must seek an answer. Even during the Holocene maximum, the winter up here would have been harsh and long. How have they managed it?

New questions are constantly emerging. Such is the case with archeology! Each discovery bring forth new mysteries that call for an answer.

It may be that I see something new when I look at the petroglyphs again. Maybe I only see it when I go through the drawings at home. There are always new questions and answers waiting.

In the distance I see some musk oxen wandering. They survived through the ice age and the Holocene maximum all the way up to today. So much the better than the other ice age giants who disappeared with the ice while the whale culture moved up the Arctic.

As the whale culture were so dependent on whales for the maintenance of their culture, it would be obvious that they have been following the whales north as the ice has retreated. Perhaps they have simply followed where their prey was most prevalent until they reached the top of the world, where the return of the ice then toke them by surprise and the long Arctic night was too long.

It is not inconceivable that the whale culture has come with the whales from the south as the ice of the ice age has retreated and the whale culture has simply followed suit.

It makes sense. It strikes me that the culture has not necessarily been suitable for the long Arctic night, as hunting from their airships has been almost impossible in the dark. They have had to gather large supplies for the winter.

Their lack of stone culture also suggests a lack of knowledge about the use of the resources of the land. Only with the downfall of their whale-based culture have they begun to use stones in the Indenpendence cultures, the Saqqaq culture, and the Dorset culture. There has been an increasing trend towards the use of land resources, as the return of the ice made whaling from airships more difficult and ultimately impossible.

But that again begs the pressing question; Where did the whale culture come from?

If, before the Holocene maximum, they have chased the whales from the ice edge, then they may have followed the ice edge northwards as it retreated and eventually, as the ice retreated all the way, they have landed on the Arctic islands to pursue their catch from there. Here they have then begun to use the cliffs to tell their story in stone. The first thing they have used stones for.

That they may have lived on the ice during the ice age may also explain the way they have made holes in the rock for their buildings. On ice, they have mounted their whale halls down into depressions in the ice and after they went ashore, they have done the same in the peat and rock, which has been more permanent but also harder to mount in. They, in turn, have been able to return to the settlement again and again as they followed the whales.

I sit down and look out over the ocean, where icebergs and drift ice float lazily by. I may be dealing here with a nautical culture that has gone ashore as the ice that they have lived on during the ice age has melted away under their feet. The idea is fantastic, but it is clear in everything I find about the whale culture that terrestrial animals have been something new and secondary, while marine animals and especially whales have been the deciding factor.

It also horribly means that this culture will be very difficult to follow and find further evidence for, as most of it will have disappeared into the sea. It is only up here, where it has finally been forced ashore under the heat of the Holocene maximum, that they will have left traces carved in rocks. Or hopefully where their lives along the ice edge have been in contact with land.

That's what I need to work on. I have to find traces of it from stories on the Arctic islands and what may have been along the coasts where the ice has reached during the ice age. That way, I will be able to trace the origins of the whale culture even further back in the darkness of the ice age.

It seems conceivable that the whale culture originated along the ice edge of the ice age oceans, where winter has been less dark and hunting from airships has been possible all year and since the ice has retreated at the end of the ice age, the whale culture has followed the ice and whales north.

This idea makes good sense to me and also explains the total lack of use of land-based resources. If the whale culture has spent the entire ice age on sea ice, then it makes sense that all of their technology would be based on the resources they have been able to get from their sea prey.

My heart fills with greater and greater curiosity. It becomes clearer to me that here I have found the first piece in a whole new and unknown chapter in human cultural history.

A culture so fundamentally different and based on the sea rather than the land. It can take human cultural history a long way back in time and show that culture has been possible in ways that are fundamentally different from the agrarian cultures to which we are accustomed from archeology.

A development of the hunter-gatherer culture which, due to the richness of the hunting basis, has been able to be far richer and more developed than hunter-gatherer cultures on land. With their airships, the whale culture has been able to dominate the entire sea along the edges of the ice.

It is curious to think that their presence here in the Arctic, which from their petroglyphs seems so established, has been a decline, where they have had to follow the ice and the whales as they pulled north and when the ice finally came back again, it was the downfall of their culture, as at that time they had gone ashore and were unable to adapt their whale-based culture to both ice and darkness.

The storm spirits from the petroglyphs have forced the whale culture to become a land and seal culture, as we eventually know it from the Dorset culture and those of their technologies that could be adapted to stone as the blubber lamp was transformed into stone. But what was dependent on plenty of whales disappeared. Their large whale halls thus became peat huts.

In this way, a culture that was suitable for ice and lighter conditions was drawn to the north, as the ice faded away, but when the ice came back, it was not able to cope with both the cold and the winter darkness. The whale culture was simply not able to keep up with the ice edge back to the south, but became trapped deep behind the ice and changed into a land and coastal culture.

It shows how dependent a culture is on the specific landscape and climatic conditions on which it is based. If those conditions disappear, so do the cultural elements.

The most famous cultures for posterity will then be those that leave the most marks in the landscape, as we know it from the Mediterranean cultures, while a culture like the whale culture will be swallowed up by the sea on which it was so dependent.

After walking around the beautiful landscape and thus letting my mind fly, I return to the cliff where the whale culture has, after all, left a mark for posterity.

I've been walking so long that it's again time to return to L'Aguila and get some sleep, but tomorrow I'll finish painting the rock and be able to make the final drawings. Everything has gone far beyond expectation, I have found more than I could have dreamed of and can look forward to having a lot to work with. My travels will in the future guide me further in my search for the past of the whale culture, so that I may be able to find its origins in the ancient times of mankind.

After sleeping and eating aboard L'Aguila, I return to the cliff that shines brightly. After yesterday's thoughts, there are several petroglyphs that used to be mysterious that now appear before me in a different light.

In particular, I now clearly see the rim that must indicate the edge of the ice, where the whalers originally lived and how they were eventually forced ashore. All the warming that had brought them to the Arctic can be interpreted as a time of recession! They have been forced north and ashore!

I work my way forward quickly and find petroglyphs showing the problem of the airships when the long arctic night falls and how depots were put down in the summer to get through the long night and the fear when the sun disappeared.

There is so much that is becoming more and more clear now that I have seen so much. It has been terrible for these people to be forced ashore and in the end it undermined their culture that they had to adapt to the land. I'm done with the rock now. Everything has been painted and I have made drawings of all the petroglyphs.

I take a step back and admire the now colorful rock that speaks to me across the millennia.

It is the irony of fate that if the whale culture had not been forced ashore and had begun to make petroglyphs, I would not have been able to find any trace of them. What became their downfall was also what made them leave a mark for posterity. Otherwise the sea would have erased everything!

I admire my work and all the beautifully chiseled petroglyphs that now appear clearly painted on the rock. They tell the story of a hitherto unknown culture that now emerges from the darkness of perdition and shows a much older and deeper origin for the Arctic cultures, which are now open to being explored and told.

For me, it will be a joy to be the one who can lay the first and hopefully more stones in this story, so that I and the whale culture can travel even further back into their primeval times to the skies from which they came and thus inscribe a whole new chapter in human cultural history.

Here I have found signs of an ocean culture that has lived its life on the resources that have been extracted from the sea and with these reached an astonishingly high technical level. The closest other culture that we know of that has been so much oriented towards the sea is the Austronesian culture that spread over Polynesia's many islands, but they went after the islands. The whale culture seems to have been oriented towards the ice and only went ashore when the ice became rare. This makes it unique in relation to other cultures, where the sea is a way of life or travel, but where you always pull ashore to shelter from the weather. But with ice, you have a kind of solid ground under your feet.

Now there is nothing left but to pack up and get all my work back on board L'Aguila. I have done a lot of work here, but in front of me is an even bigger job in getting an overview of all the drawings that I have made and preparing my next trip to Svalbard to examine the stories that I have found about rocks with petroglyphs there. It might give me an idea of where the whale culture and all its secrets came from before it reached the east coast of Greenland.

Back on L'Aguila, I get everything packed down well and start getting ready to lift anchor. There is a nice offshore breeze that I can set sail to use to get out of the fjord and home. Then I also save some fuel and engine power. There is something special about riding the wind.

As I sail drowsily out of the fjord, I look back towards the coast and up the cliff, where I can see my color work. That rock is the last of the whale culture, but the first in my travels to find this unique and forgotten culture, which is the origin of later Arctic cultures, but which has been forgotten because it has left so little impact and its remains has been engulfed by the sea on which the culture has been so dependent.

Outside the fjord I catch the wind and start south. On my route home I will make stops in Scoresbysund, Reykjavik and Thorshavn en route to Myland.

Then I can start working on my upcoming travels and doing my work regarding the whale culture and its possible origins.

To the starboard side, the Greenlandic coast glides calmly past me with all its hidden mysteries. What else can hide here among the mountains of oblivion? Could there be more rocks like the one I just painted? Later studies might clarify this so that the secrets can be snatched away from the landscape and tell archeology about forgotten ages waiting to be found.